Text copyright © 2004 by Ana Maria Machado
Illustrations copyright © 2004 by Laurent Cardon
Graphic design © 2004 by Sylvain Barré
English translation copyright © 2010 by Elisa Amado
Originally published as *Procura-se lobo* by Editora Ática in Brazil
in 2005.
First published in English in Canada and the USA in 2010 by
Groundwood Books.
Second printing 2010

Groundwood Books / House of Anansi Press
110 Spadina Avenue, Suite 801, Toronto, Ontario M5V 2K4
or c/o Publishers Group West
1700 Fourth Street, Berkeley, CA 94710

We acknowledge for their financial support of our publishing
program the Canada Council for the Arts, the Government of
Canada through the Canada Book Fund (CBF) and the Ontario
Arts Council.

**Canada Council   Conseil des Arts
for the Arts   du Canada**

**ONTARIO ARTS COUNCIL
CONSEIL DES ARTS DE L'ONTARIO**

Library and Archives Canada Cataloguing in Publication
Machado, Ana Maria
Wolf wanted / Ana Maria Machado ; illustrator, Laurent Cardon ;
translator, Elisa Amado.

Translation of: Procura-se lobo.
ISBN 978-0-88899-880-4

1. Wolves–Juvenile fiction.
I. Amado, Elisa II. Cardon, Laurent III. Title.

PZ7.M1795W64 2009   j869.3'42   C2009-905359-4

Graphic design by Sylvain Barré
Printed and bound in China

PHOTO CREDITS
Corbis: Ethiopian wolf, Martin Harvey; Iberian wolf, Terry
    Whittaker/Frank Lane Picture Agency.
Getty Images: Arctic wolf, Frank Lukasseck/Photographer's Choice;
    Coyote, Gail Shumway/Taxi; Dingo, Chris Sattlberger/Image
    Bank; Golden jackal, Tom Brakefield/Photodisc; Gray wolf,
    Joseph Van Os/Image Bank; Red fox, Andrew Davies/Flickr; Red
    wolf, Gary Randall/Taxi.

ANA MARIA MACHADO

WOLF WANTED

LAURENT CARDON

Translated by Elisa Amado

GROUNDWOOD BOOKS
HOUSE OF ANANSI PRESS
TORONTO   BERKELEY

Manny was looking for a job. He opened the paper and saw:

Wolf Wanted

A good-looking adult, with experience, for a responsible position. Well paid. Future guaranteed. Send a CV and a letter describing expectations to this newspaper.

Manny doubted that wolves could read the paper. Or that they would understand anything about CVs or expectations. But he did.

A CV is a list of everything you've ever done that might help you get a job.

As for expectations, well, sometimes people have very high expectations and might even think that they are too good for a job. But in this case Manny knew that expectations meant what do you expect to get paid?

He knew all about job ads and what the words in them meant. He had been looking for a job for quite a while and had read quite a few of them.

Manny was a Wolf but he wasn't a wolf. He was a person. Just like other people whose last names are the same as certain animals — Coyote, Lamb, Peacock — his last name was Wolf. Manny Wolf. So he decided it was worth trying his luck. And he answered the ad, as though the company that placed it wanted to hire someone whose name was Wolf.

It wasn't a bad idea. But in fact the company wanted a real wolf — an animal that was hairy with four legs, like a big dog.

This turned out to be lucky for Manny. A few days later he received a letter from the company asking him to come by their office because they needed someone.

In fact he was precisely the one they needed.

Many wolves had responded to the ad. The company had received many letters. Too many. So many they had to create a new job — they needed a person to answer the letters from the wolves. And they wanted Manny to do this job. It was because he had written them such a good letter, you know. They really liked his letter.

Mr. Manny Wolf
Department of
Human Resources

Manny's writing skills turned out to solve his biggest problem — finding a job. Lucky he was such a good writer.

But even better, Manny Wolf loved to read. He knew lots of stories. And because of that there wasn't a wolf around who could fool such a reader as he. All he had to do was to start reading a letter and he could see right through it.

The first letter started like this:

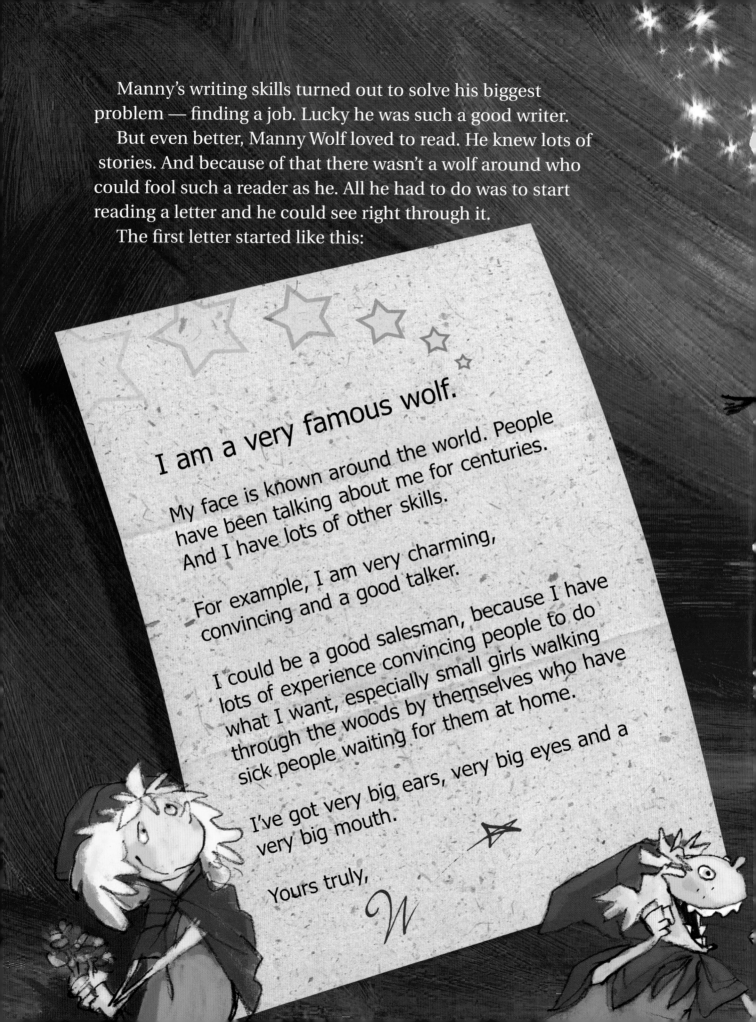

I am a very famous wolf.

My face is known around the world. People have been talking about me for centuries. And I have lots of other skills.

For example, I am very charming, convincing and a good talker.

I could be a good salesman, because I have lots of experience convincing people to do what I want, especially small girls walking through the woods by themselves who have sick people waiting for them at home.

I've got very big ears, very big eyes and a very big mouth.

Yours truly,

W

NO MORE APPLICATIONS

Manny Wolf replied:

**DEPARTMENT OF
HUMAN RESOURCES**

Esteemed Sir,

Sadly, we don't need someone who can hear better, see better or eat better. Our hunting department suggests you seek employment in a storybook, especially in "Little Red Riding Hood." There might be a vacancy because the wolf in that story comes to a bad end.

Sincerely,

Manny Wolf

Manny Wolf

The second job seeker got straight to the point:

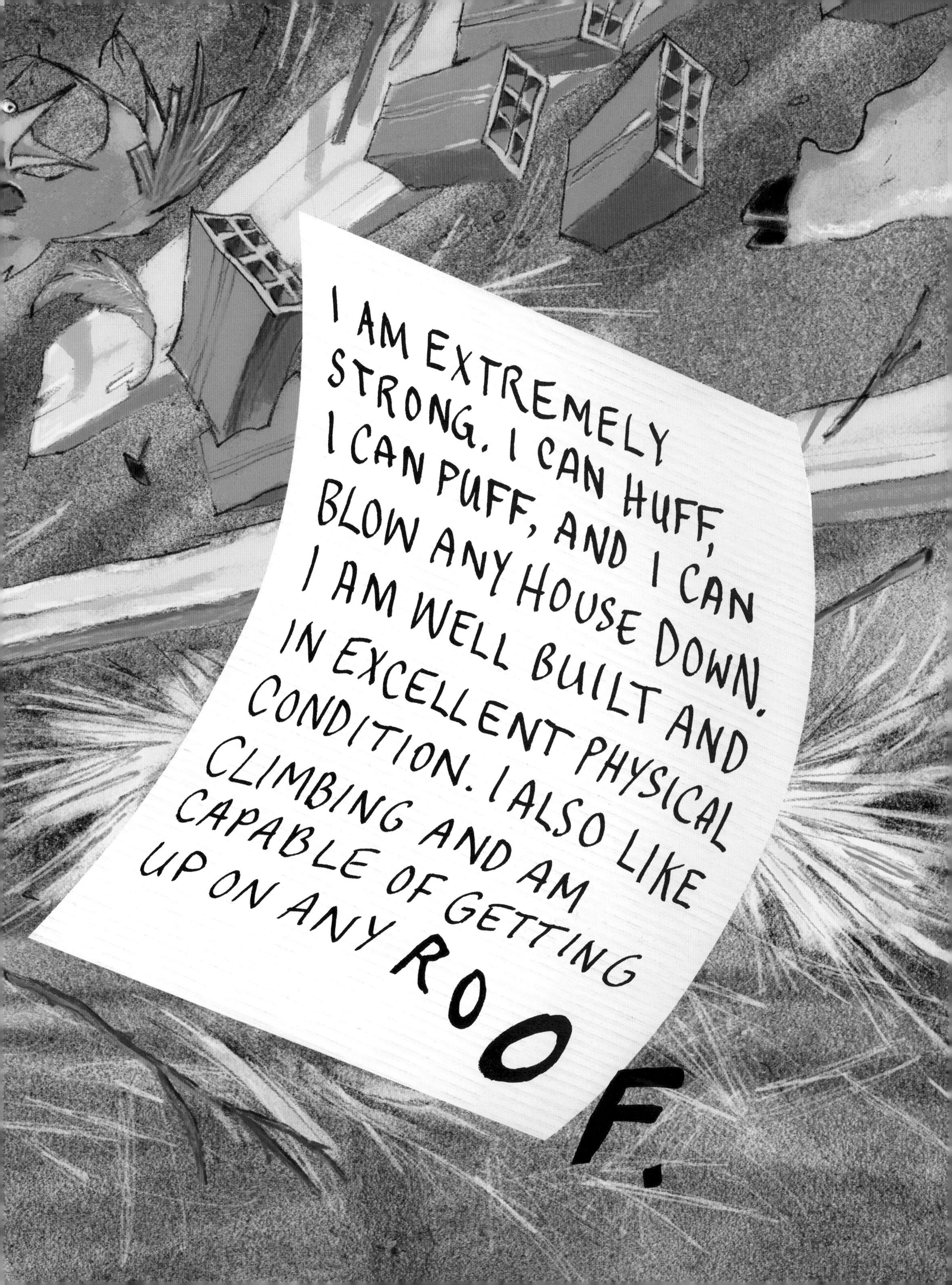
I AM EXTREMELY STRONG. I CAN HUFF, I CAN PUFF, AND I CAN BLOW ANY HOUSE DOWN. I AM WELL BUILT AND IN EXCELLENT PHYSICAL CONDITION. I ALSO LIKE CLIMBING AND AM CAPABLE OF GETTING UP ON ANY ROOF.

The response from Manny Wolf was polite but firm:

Mr. Wolf,

Three brothers who happen to work in our building department already forwarded your references to us. We know you have trouble keeping appointments, and we can't afford to hire someone who is always late for meetings. Sadly, we don't have time to wait for you. We suggest you look for work in a storybook. There seems to be a vacancy in "The Three Little Pigs" because the wolf in that story comes to a bad end.

Sincerely,

Manny Wolf

Manny Wolf

The third applicant didn't supply very much information. He only stated that he had a good record as a night watchman, and that he always knew when someone had gone out and left their children at home alone. Even better, he said he could supply excellent references as long as no one asked the seven little kids about him.

Manny Wolf soon figured out who this wolf was. He tried to send him off to a story, too. You must have guessed — it was to "The Wolf and the Seven Little Kids."

The next two letters looked a lot alike. Were they written by two wolves or one? The handwriting was almost identical, and the letters were on the same kind of paper.

The first was written in a very gentle, agreeable way:

I can fit into any environment very well. It takes me no time at all to become just like everyone else around me. I don't stick out in any way. I'm happy to wear any kind of clothes for my work. Nothing bothers me. In fact I love to disguise myself.

But the next sounded quite different:

You will have to hire me, because you owe it to me. Last year you held a competition. I am certain that I won, and yet you didn't call me. And if it wasn't you who didn't call, it was your brother. And if you don't have a brother, it must have been your father. And if your father was traveling, it must have been your son. And if you don't call me right away, I'll eat everyone and finish this farce off once and for all.

Manny Wolf sighed. He quickly typed very polite replies on his computer, printed them out and sealed them in two separate envelopes.

To Mr. Wolf in sheep's clothing

AESOP'S FABLES

Next he opened two completely unoriginal letters.
They were really just notes:

I am a Big Bad Wolf,
a Big Bad Wolf,
a Big Bad Wolf.

Who's afraid of
the Big Bad Wolf,
the Big Bad Wolf,
the Big Bad Wolf?

Manny Wolf recognized these applicants right away and knew that they were pretending to be someone else, hoping for another chance.

He could understand that. He himself had looked for a job for a long time and he knew you had to keep trying. But he wasn't about to waste his time writing new letters to the same animals. To show that he understood what they were up to, he returned the notes, one with his letter to the Little Red Riding Hood wolf, and the other with his letter to the Three Little Pigs wolf.

The next wolf sent such a badly scrawled letter, filled with crossed-out words, that Manny Wolf couldn't understand a thing it said. He could only make out the signature — Wolfling. He thought maybe it had come from a rock-and-roll singer who had written in a hurry while playing the guitar or the drums without even putting the paper down on something to keep it flat. But then he noticed there was a P.S. down below the signature:

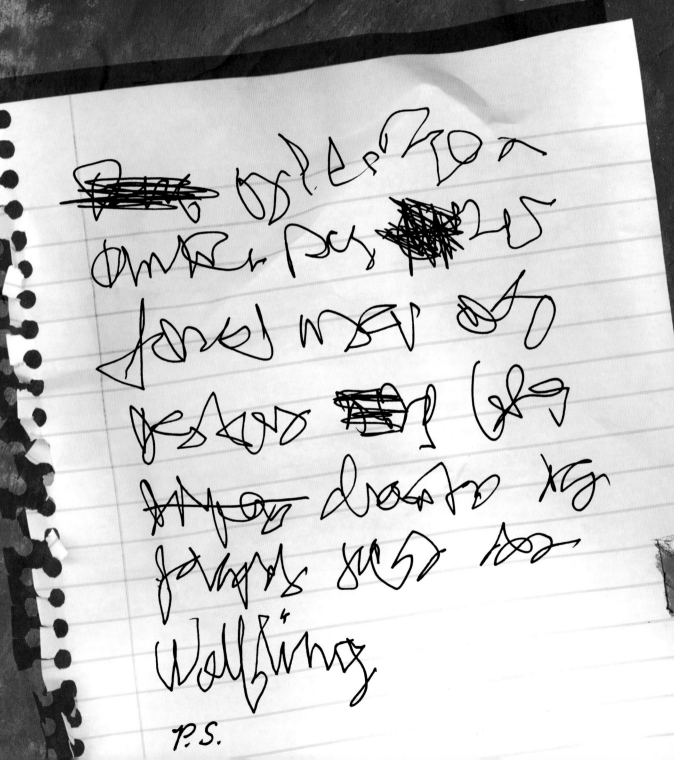

P.S.

I apologize. My father didn't go to school and that's why he can't write straight. But I can. And I don't want this job — not at all — because I'm going to school. Some day I hope I can get a much better job.

Little Wolfling

Oh! Now Manny Wolf understood. He knew this father and son from the comics and cartoons. And he knew there was no point in writing a long letter because the "Wolfling" wouldn't be able to read it. So he just answered with a brief note:

The next letter was much more original. Finally, a different kind of wolf had appeared — a creature who was neither bad, nor ate people. On the contrary, he presented himself as having outstanding qualities:

I am brave and courageous. I have lots of friends. We live together in a pack and are very close. I am also an excellent head of my family. I have lots of experience in education and have helped to bring up other people's children. If you need references, please contact the bear Baloo, the panther Bagheera, or the boy Mowgli. I'm sure they will confirm that I am a good father and that my teaching has produced good results.

Manny Wolf knew that he had to find a real wolf, not a character from a book. But he couldn't bring himself to say no to such a generous and appealing wolf. He put the letter aside, saying, I'll talk to the boss later. Who knows, maybe we can find a spot for this one, too. He might do, even if only as a role model.

And the next letter? Unlike the rest it came from a Mrs. Wolf.
And unlike the rest it was hard to tell if she was a character in
a book or made up. Manny Wolf had already heard her
mentioned with a great deal of respect.
Lots of people were certain
she was real.

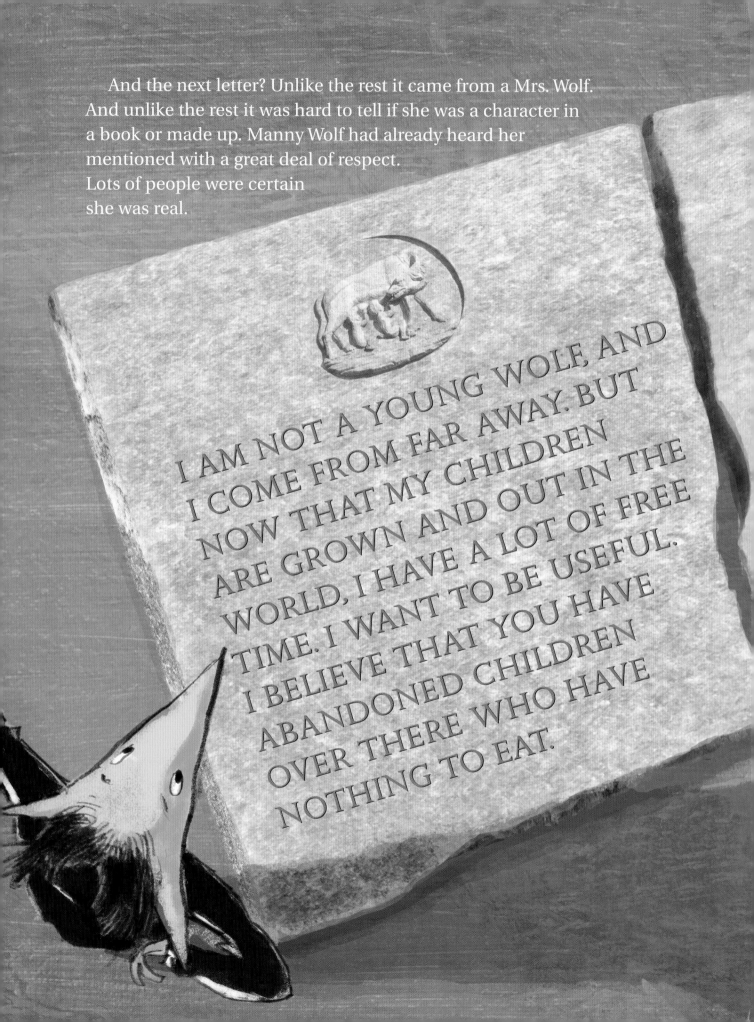

I AM NOT A YOUNG WOLF, AND
I COME FROM FAR AWAY. BUT
NOW THAT MY CHILDREN
ARE GROWN AND OUT IN THE
WORLD, I HAVE A LOT OF FREE
TIME. I WANT TO BE USEFUL.
I BELIEVE THAT YOU HAVE
ABANDONED CHILDREN
OVER THERE WHO HAVE
NOTHING TO EAT.

MAYBE THAT IS WHY YOU ARE LOOKING FOR WOLVES, BECAUSE YOU KNOW FOR SURE THAT WE WOULD NEVER ABANDON OUR BABIES. I CAN BREASTFEED. MY GOOD MILK HAS ALREADY FED TWO STRONG BOYS, ROMULUS AND REMUS. ONE OF THEM FOUNDED ROME.

Manny knew that this was not the wolf they were looking for, but he couldn't bring himself to dispense with Mrs. Wolf's services just like that. He sent her the addresses of some places where she might be welcome. She might, for example, pose for sculptors or people making coins. Sadly, since there was no lack of abandoned children in the world, maybe she could teach people something and have a brilliant future.

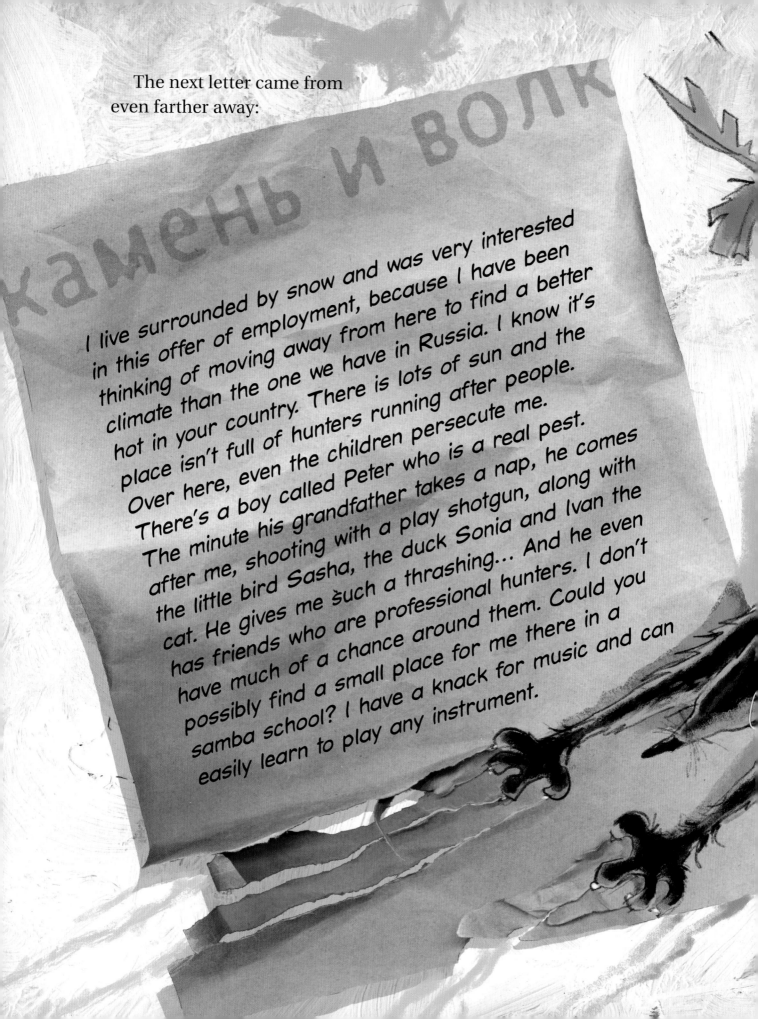

The next letter came from even farther away:

I live surrounded by snow and was very interested in this offer of employment, because I have been thinking of moving away from here to find a better climate than the one we have in Russia. I know it's hot in your country. There is lots of sun and the place isn't full of hunters running after people. Over here, even the children persecute me. There's a boy called Peter who is a real pest. The minute his grandfather takes a nap, he comes after me, shooting with a play shotgun, along with the little bird Sasha, the duck Sonia and Ivan the cat. He gives me such a thrashing... And he even has friends who are professional hunters. I don't have much of a chance around them. Could you possibly find a small place for me there in a samba school? I have a knack for music and can easily learn to play any instrument.

Manny Wolf read and read and answered and answered, but the pile of letters was still huge. He found a letter from a wolf who howled at the moon, one from a mysterious wolf of the steppes, another from a wolf who ran with women, and another from a wolf who chased sleds. There were even letters from werewolves.

Manny Wolf answered each one. But not one of the candidates was right for the job. Not even the one who was friends with a saint and had marvelous references:

You can see my portrait on altars and in stained-glass windows. My name is the Wolf of Gubbio. I was belligerent and greedy, but not out of malice. It was because I was hungry. One very cold winter, when I had nothing to eat, I attacked the city of Gubbio in Italy. But when Francis of Assisi fed me, I became very gentle and from then on we were great friends. What a saintly man!

It hurt to turn down such a wolf.
But he wasn't what was wanted.

Tired from answering so many letters, Manny Wolf began to think that all of this would never end.

Then at last he realized what the problem was. The advertisement wasn't clear. It didn't say what kind of wolf they were looking for, nor why they wanted one. The ad must have been written by someone who couldn't write!

Manny had an idea.

Why don't we place another ad, a clearer one.

And so the next day, the following ad appeared in the paper:

Wanted — A Real Wolf

An animal who can't read and doesn't appear in a book. If you know where to find one, let us know and we will compensate you. You might even become part of our team. We want to make a documentary about wolves for television. We want to show the viewers their behavior, their habits, how they live, what they like, what their environments are like, what endangers them. We want to defend their natural way of life and ensure that these animals have a future, because right now they are in danger of extinction. Send replies to this newspaper.

Some letters came. Many of them were from children. They described wolves and their relatives in different countries, in forest reserves, in mountainous areas, in desert regions. In Brazil there was the guará wolf. In North America, the gray wolf. None of these wolves needed a job. But they all needed to be protected. That's why many of them became television stars.

With all this information it was easy. Manny Wolf joined the television crew and now he has a new job. He travels around the world studying animals and making documentaries about them. And he does a very good job because, after all, he is a human whose last name is Wolf.

Arctic Wolf (Canis lupus arctos)
The arctic wolf's white fur provides good camouflage against the snow. It hunts over a vast territory to find its prey. The main prey of the arctic wolf are musk oxen and arctic hare.

Gray Wolf (Canis lupus)
In 1974 the gray wolf was declared an endangered species in the United States. Since then the species has made a comeback in many areas, and some farmers are once again concerned about their livestock. In some states the gray wolf has been removed from endangered species lists, and they are at risk from hunters once again.

Coyote (Canis latrans)
Coyotes are smaller than wolves. They are found throughout most of North America and Central America. Small animals such as mice and rabbits make up a large part of their diet.

Red Wolf (Canis rufus)
The red wolf is a critically endangered species. But since 1988, when scientists reintroduced red wolves in captivity into the wild, their numbers have grown.

Wolves and Their Relatives

Wolves, along with coyotes, jackals, foxes and dogs, belong to a family of animals known as *Canidae*, or the dog family. Most scientists agree that there are only two species of wolves: the gray wolf (*Canis lupus*), which lives in North America, Europe and Asia, and the red wolf (*Canis rufus*), found only in North Carolina in the eastern United States. There are a variety of types, or subspecies, of the gray wolf. Scientists are studying the Ethiopian wolf (*Canis simensis*) to determine if it is a wolf species or a type of jackal.

For many years humans have poisoned, trapped and shot wolves, either out of fear or to protect their farm animals. But science tells us that the wolf plays an important role in ecosystems. When humans allow wolves to live in an area, the health of their prey populations improves. We are now much more aware of preserving wolves, but wolves and their relatives are still at risk in some parts of the world.

Guará Wolf or Maned Wolf (Chrysocyon brachyurus)
In spite of its name, the guará wolf is not a true wolf, but it does belong to the dog family. It is an omnivore, feasting on fruit and small animals. It is currently threatened by loss of habitat and hunting. The guará wolf is found in Peru, Bolivia, Paraguay, Uruguay, Argentina and Brazil. It is legally protected in Brazil.

Red Fox (*Vulpes vulpes*)
Red foxes are found all over the world. They do well in many different habitats, both in the wild and in populated areas. They are solitary hunters and carnivores that eat small mammals, but they also scavenge on fruit and garbage.

Golden Jackal (*Canis aureus*)
The golden jackal is an omnivore and a scavenger. It is found in India, the Middle East, Southeast Europe and Africa. There are two other kinds of jackals that live only in Africa — the side-striped jackal and the black-backed jackal.

Iberian Wolf (*Canis lupus signatus*)
The Iberian wolf lives in the mountains and countryside of northwestern Spain and northern Portugal. It preys on deer, wild boar and farm animals.

Ethiopian Wolf (*Canis simensis*)
This rare carnivore lives in the high country of Ethiopia, where it hunts alpine rats. Its young are born with their eyes closed, and they cannot see or hear for the first few weeks. This animal's population is dropping due to habitat loss, hunting and disease. It is fully protected by Ethiopia's Wildlife Conservation Regulations.

Dingo (*Canis lupus dingo*)
This wild dog lives in Australia. It was probably introduced to the country by traders from Asia thousands of years ago. In packs, dingoes are capable of hunting animals as large as kangaroos. But they also often hunt alone.